Four Cheese Murder

Book Seven

in

Papa Pacelli's

Pizzeria Series

By

Patti Benning

Author's Note: On the next page, you'll find out how to access all of my books easily, as well as locate books by best-selling author, Summer Prescott. I'd love to hear your thoughts on my books, the storylines, and anything else that you'd like to comment on – reader feedback is very important to me. Please see the following page for my publisher's contact information. If you'd like to be on her list of "folks to contact" with updates, release and sales notifications, etc…just shoot her an email and let her know. Thanks for reading!

Also…

…if you're looking for more great reads, from me and Summer, check out the Summer Prescott Publishing Book Catalog:

http://summerprescottbooks.com/book-catalog/ for some truly delicious stories.

Contact Info for Summer Prescott Publishing:

Twitter: @summerprescott1

Blog and Book Catalog: http://summerprescottbooks.com

Email: summer.prescott.cozies@gmail.com

And...look up The Summer Prescott Fan Page on Facebook – let's be friends!

If you're an author and are interested in publishing with Summer Prescott Books – please send Summer an email and she'll send you submission guidelines.

TABLE OF CONTENTS

FOUR CHEESE
MURDER

Book Seven in Papa Pacelli's Pizzeria Series

CHAPTER ONE

"Thanks for choosing Papa Pacelli's. Have a nice day!"

Eleanora Pacelli waved at the customer as she drove away, then pulled the drive-up window shut. It was cold outside, the sort of cold that made her skin hurt and the breath catch in her lungs. She was surprised that the pizzeria was as busy as they had been today. She supposed a lot of that had to do with the fact that her customers no longer had to get out of the car to pick up a pizza, now that the drive-up window was installed. It certainly did make handing off orders easier and quicker, though she could have done without the blast of cold air through the kitchen whenever the window was opened.

She was ready for winter to be over and done with. With the holidays already past, there seemed to be nothing to look forward to but months of cold, dreary weather. She wanted to be able to go outside without wearing what felt like a hundred layers. She wanted to be able to lay in the sun on her family's boat again, and go on long walks with her dog without slipping on ice and stumbling through snow drifts.

I love Kittiport, she thought. *I just hate Kittiport in winter.* Overall, she was still tremendously glad that she had made the decision to move to Maine after her old life in Chicago imploded. She was getting to know her grandmother, a woman that she had barely seen since she was a teenager; and had somehow ended up first managing, and now owning the family restaurant. Not only that, but she had begun a relationship with an amazing man.

Russell Ward was the sheriff of Kittiport. His job kept him busy, but she didn't mind. She knew how much he cared about the citizens that he protected, and she admired that about him greatly. Of course, dating the sheriff in a small town meant that more than a few people knew about their relationship, and she wasn't sure whether she was better known as the lady who owned the pizza place, or the lady who was dating Sheriff Ward.

Papa Pacelli's was famous enough in its own right. The business was over twenty years old, and was a favorite place to eat for people of all ages. The pizza they served was the best she had ever had, and she wasn't just saying that because she made them. They offered everything from proper deep dish to the weird thin crust so inexplicably beloved by easterners, and had even started serving calzones a few months back. The pizzeria kept a stock of all of the normal toppings, but also had a special pizza of the week that often had more exotic toppings or unusual combinations.

Ellie was proud to be part of the business that her grandfather had started. He was no longer here to see it, but she was sure he would approve of what she had done with the place. Her grandmother sure seemed to. Ann Pacelli, now almost fully recovered from the broken arm she had received a few months before, had begun coming in to help out around the pizzeria once or twice a week. She spent most of her time out front, ringing people up or just chatting with the customers, and had become something of a mascot around the place. Ellie worried about her constantly—the older woman seemed convinced that she could do anything someone half her age could do, and acted accordingly—but she was also glad that her grandmother was still so active. Besides, everyone loved her.

"Hey Ms. Pacelli," Jacob, her delivery driver, said as he came in through the employee entrance. He was wearing a parka zipped up to his throat and a warm hat. Ellie felt for him, having to go out in the cold to make deliveries, but he promised that he didn't mind it. People tended to give better tips when the weather was bad, so she believed him.

"Hi Jacob," she said. "The next order isn't quite ready yet. You should warm up and get something to eat. Do you want a calzone?"

"Sure," he said. "Thanks."

Her employees always ate free. It was a policy that her grandfather had implemented since his first day of business, and Ellie planned to keep it in place for as long as she was in charge. Papa Pacelli's depended on its employees to be hardworking and reliable. Offering them free meals was the least she could do to show her gratitude.

Just as the calzone was about to come out of the oven, another one of her employees came in. She shut the door quickly behind her and pulled down her hood to reveal a head of bushy brown hair.

"Sorry I'm late," Clara said, shaking the snow off of her gloves before pulling them off. "I stopped by the community center on my way over, and got lost in conversation with one of the women volunteering there."

"You're fine," Ellie said. "According to this clock, you're on time, and it's the one that counts." The kitchen clock was slow, something that she had been meaning to fix for a while but had never gotten around to. "What's going on at the community center?"

"A group of volunteers is hosting a drive to collect blankets, food, hats, gloves, and scarves for people who need help," the young woman said. "I had a bunch of old winter stuff that I decided to donate."

"Do they need more? The pizzeria could donate some pizzas, and I know my grandmother has boxes and boxes of old clothing and blankets that no one ever uses."

"Definitely. A lot of people lost power during the storm the other night. I think they can use all the help they can get."

"I'll stop there on my way home and talk to someone. Who should I ask for when I get there?"

"Oh, any of the volunteers could help you," Clara said. "I think some guy named Ronald is in charge of the programs there, but if he isn't in you can just talk to whoever's around."

It will feel good to give back to the community, Ellie thought as she pulled her coat on an hour later and prepared to leave for the day. She had already double-checked the hours that the community center was open, and she had plenty of time. Kittiport was an amazing town, and she was happy to find a way to say thank you.

CHAPTER TWO

Ellie left the community center that evening with a sense of purpose. The man she had spoken to had been a little bit odd and distant at first, but when he heard she wanted to donate not just old blankets, but food, he had warmed right up. She had gone on a tour of the building, which was currently acting as a sort of impromptu soup kitchen and shelter for those who had nowhere warm to stay during the cold weather. She hadn't realized just how many people had been affected by the extreme cold, and felt bad for not doing anything sooner.

She and her grandmother must have gotten luckier than they knew during the storm that had blown through town a few days ago. Their power had hardly even flickered, though even if it had gone out, they would have been able to use the fireplace to keep warm. The large house was a few miles outside of town, sandwiched between the coast and the forest of a large state park. Ellie, who had grown up in Chicago, wasn't used to having so much wilderness literally in her back yard. She had felt isolated at first, but was beginning to enjoy the peace and quiet that the big house offered.

"Nonna, I'm home," she called as she let herself in the front door.

The sound of tiny claws clacking on the hard floor announced the presence of Bunny, her little black and white Papillon. Ellie crouched down just as the dog rounded the corner and caught the bundle of fur in her arms.

"Hey, now, I missed you too," she said, trying to get the dog to calm down. "I'll never understand why you act like this every time I come home. I know for a fact Nonna sneaks you food while I'm not here; you should be happy to see me leave for work in the mornings."

"Oh, she is," Nonna said, following the dog much more slowly into the foyer. "After she does her little bit with you and watches you leave, she comes trotting right into the kitchen and plants herself by the pantry. She knows she gets a morning treat while I drink my coffee. If I forget, she gives me the same pitiful look she gives you when you're putting on your boots. She knows we're putty in her little paws if she can make us feel bad enough for her."

"I never knew that," Ellie said, laughing. "She sure is spoiled. I'm glad she's such a happy little dog."

"She's quite the character," Nonna said with a smile. "How is everything going at the pizzeria? Have you started serving that grain-free pizza yet?"

"It's gluten free, Nonna, and no, I'm waiting on the new menus to come in."

"I still don't quite understand the point of it, but I'm glad you're keeping up with the times. Everyone at physical therapy was thrilled to learn that my granddaughter was the owner of Papa Pacelli's. You should come sometime."

After getting her cast off, Nonna had been assigned to a month of physical therapy to help retrain the muscles in her arm. Ellie was still shaken by the entire experience—a broken bone was no small thing at her grandmother's age. The older woman seemed to be taking everything in good humor, though. She enjoyed any excuse to get out of the house, even if that meant spending a grueling forty minutes doing stretches and lifting weights under the practiced eye of a physical therapist.

"You make it sound like I'm some sort of celebrity," Ellie said with a smile. "There are a lot of small business owners around here. Besides, Papa's the one that deserves all of the credit."

"Oh, you know you've done a lot for the pizzeria, Ellie. People can see the difference, and they like it. Such a popular restaurant is good for the entire town."

The pizzeria owner decided to change the subject. She didn't feel that she deserved the credit her grandmother was trying to give her. "Speaking of being good for the entire town, there's a winter clothes and food drive going on at the community center that I thought the pizzeria could get involved in. We could donate some of the old clothes and blankets in the basement, and I can donate a few pizzas. What do you think?"

"That's a wonderful idea. Art used to donate to some of the charity drives," Nonna said. She narrowed her eyes. "In fact, I think a couple of the boxes in the basement might have items he planned to donate and never got around to actually bringing in. I'm glad you brought it up, or I never would have remembered. I'm sure he'd be happy to see the donations go to charity at last."

"I'll dig through the boxes and bring up any of the ones that look promising," Ellie said. "But first I want to say hi to Marlowe and grab a snack."

Marlowe was a green-winged macaw that her grandfather had bought when he retired. The parrot was one of the most complicated pets Ellie had ever known. Not only was she temperamental at times, but she could talk, and didn't hesitate to make her desires known. Caring for the bird was much different than caring for Bunny. The little dog might find her way into trouble sometimes, but at least she didn't have a beak that was strong enough to break bones and tear through a wall.

The big red parrot greeted her with an exuberant "Hi!" when she saw her. Ellie reached into the basket that they kept stored under the cage and grabbed an almond, still in its in shell. She opened the cage and Marlowe climbed out on top, keeping an eager eye on the almond.

"This is for you," Ellie said. "Can you say please?"

The bird looked at her.

"Come on, say please."

"Thank you!" Marlowe squawked.

Ellie laughed. "Close enough." She handed the almond over and watched as the bird effortlessly cracked the shell to get to the nut inside. She was still a little bit afraid of that beak, but overall, she was pleased at how well her relationship with Marlowe was doing. When she had first moved back, the bird hadn't wanted anything to do with her.

After watching the parrot eat her treat, she whistled to Bunny to follow her and headed down the basement stairs. Going through the boxes down there would be a time-consuming task, but at least it would be an interesting one. Her grandparents had lived in this house for decades, and some of the stuff down there was probably almost as old as she was.

CHAPTER THREE

The next day, Ellie left for work early, having stuffed two big boxes of winter clothes and blankets into the back of her car. There were even more boxes full of items for donation waiting in the foyer at home—she just hadn't been able to fit everything in her car at once. Between these first two boxes and the pizzas she was planning to make and bring over before the pizzeria opened, the community center should be set for a few days at least.

It was another icy cold day with grey clouds hanging low over the marina. She looked out to sea as she drove into town and wondered if another storm was brewing. It had been an odd winter, with the temperature changing drastically over the span of just a few days. In the last two weeks alone they had had rain, sleet, and snow. She hoped there would be another thaw soon, but if the weather changed again shortly after, that might just serve to make the roads and sidewalks even more icy and dangerous. She didn't know how much more winter this poor little town could take.

After parking her car in the lot behind the pizzeria, she locked the vehicle and let herself in the employee entrance. The pizzeria always felt so peaceful when she was the only one there, and today was no exception. There was something that Ellie loved about the restaurant when it was dark and quiet and empty, something she couldn't put into words. It was like watching a favorite pet sleep.

"Time to wake up," she said aloud as she reached for the light switch. The overhead lights flickered to life. It would be a few hours until Papa Pacelli's opened for business so she didn't bother turning on any of the lights in the front room. She just wanted to whip up a few pizzas to donate before the real work day started.

She turned on the ovens and opened the dough fridge. She peered at the neatly arranged balls of dough for a moment, trying to decide what to make. Thin crust or deep dish? What toppings? She didn't want to do anything too boring, but she also didn't want to risk putting any unpopular toppings on. She decided to make a few different types, and people could choose what they wanted. Four cheese, deep dish, veggies with white sauce, and classic pepperoni... with a variety like that, everyone was sure to find something they liked.

Making pizzas was something Ellie simply enjoyed. Even if the pizzeria burned down tomorrow and they never rebuilt, she thought she would still probably make pizza for herself and Nonna a couple of times a week. Her grandfather's original dough recipe was what really made the pizzas from Papa Pacelli's stand out, though she was sure their practice of using only high-quality, natural and—when possible—local ingredients made a difference too. She liked to think that even if there were more competition in the area, Papa Pacelli's would be able to hold its own with no problem.

She didn't skimp out on the pizzas she was making to donate. They wouldn't be making any money off of them, but that was no reason to bake substandard pies. Besides, anyone who was taking advantage of the food drive could probably use a good quality meal. By the time Clara and Rose arrived to start their shift, Ellie had a stack of ten large pizzas ready and waiting on the counter.

"What do you think?" she asked Clara. "When I asked about how much food they could use, the person I spoke to, Ronald, just said that they would appreciate whatever I could bring. I have no idea how many people need to be fed."

"Ten pizzas should go a long way," Clara said. "From what I saw yesterday, there was a steady stream of people visiting the community center, but they weren't completely packed. This should last them a while."

"Good. I'll run all of this over, then come back and help out for a bit. We should be getting a shipment of the new menus in today—can one of you send me a text if we get it while I'm gone?"

"Sure thing," Rose said. "I'll let you know."

With the boxes of clothing in the back and the pizza in the front passenger seat, Ellie's little car was full to the brim. The community center wasn't far, which was a good thing since the stack of pizza boxes was decidedly unstable. She pulled into the parking lot with one hand on the wheel and the other supporting the stack of pizzas. She grabbed one of the boxes of clothes from the back and made her way up towards the building.

"Thanks," she said when an unseen person opened the door for her. She entered carefully, hardly able to see over the top of the box. A sweet-looking woman with mouse-brown hair appeared from behind the door. She kicked down the door stop deftly with one foot to hold it open, then reached out to take the box from her.

"Are these donations?" she asked.

"Yes, and I've got more in the car," Ellie said.

"Wonderful. I'll take these to the back, and send someone out to help you."

A minute later, Ronald, the person that Ellie had originally spoken to about the donations, appeared. He made a beeline over to her and gave her a quick wave.

"Hi," he said. "Courtney said you could use some help?"

"I've got another box of clothes, plus a bunch of pizzas," she told him. "I didn't want to try bringing all of the pizzas up at once—I was afraid I'd drop them."

"Right, I'll grab those, you get the box."

Together they carried the rest of the donations and the food inside. Ellie followed Ronald to the back, where a few volunteers were sorting donations. A long table was set up at one end of the room, with a lonely bag of potato chips, a water heater, and a selection of instant teas and hot cocoa. It was here that Ronald deposited the pizzas. He cracked open the top one and gave an approving nod.

"Looks good," he said. "Papa Pacelli's is great. It's nice of you to buy these for us."

"Actually, I own the place," she said with a smile. "Consider them a donation directly from Papa Pacelli's."

"Did I hear that right?" The woman with the mouse-colored hair had reappeared. "I thought you looked familiar. I stop in there sometimes when I'm too tired to cook dinner. My name's Courtney."

"Ellie," the pizzeria owner said, shaking her hand. "It's nice to meet you. Do you work here?"

"I'm just a volunteer," Courtney said. "There aren't many paid positions. I'd love to, though, if one ever opened up. Ronald's one of the lucky ones, he's been working here for years."

Ellie turned to look at the man who had helped her, but he was gone. It seemed odd that he would just vanish without saying anything, but Ellie figured he hadn't wanted to interrupt her conversation with the other woman.

"So, is this your first time donating for one of our charity drives?" Courtney continued. "I don't think I've seen you around before."

"It is. I just moved to town around the end of summer, so there's still a lot I have to discover about Kittiport. I didn't even know the center did anything like this. I thought it was just for community events and weddings and stuff like that."

"Oh, we do everything here," Courtney said. "In the summer, we organize day camps for kids, which is fun, and sometime in the spring we'll have an adoptable pets day where the local animal shelters all bring out some of their long-term residents and try to find them homes."

"That sounds wonderful. Maybe I'll volunteer this year if I have the time."

"We'd love the help. Our team is kind of rag-tag, but people are nice for the most part. I know everyone here. That woman with the black hair is Tina, my roommate. There's Jason, our janitor. He's also the one who dresses up as Santa for the kids over the holidays. The redhead in the corner is my best friend, Kristy, and then of course you already met Ronald. There are a few more people that come and go as we need them, but this is the core team. If you want to know more about volunteering or what donations we need for the winter food and clothes drive, any one of us would be able to help."

"This seems like such a wonderful way to spend your spare time," Ellie said. "I've got a few more boxes of clothes and blankets at home, so when I bring those by I'll talk with you more about volunteering at one of the events later this year."

"Please do. It's always nice to see new people get involved with the community."

Ellie left the community center feeling happy and refreshed. It was wonderful to see so many people helping others out of the goodness of their hearts. She was glad that Clara had told her about the food and clothing drive, or else she would never have heard of it. She decided to make a point of seeking out Courtney the next time she stopped in to drop off donations—she liked the sound of the adoptable pets day in the spring, and thought that it would be a good idea to sign up as a volunteer sooner rather than later.

CHAPTER FOUR

Ellie had planned on staying only a few hours at the pizzeria, but the shipment of new menus arrived shortly after she returned. That meant that they were ready to start rolling out their newest option; gluten-free thin crust pizza.

It might have made more sense to wait until the next day and announce it properly, but Ellie decided to give the new menus a test run then and there. She had had a large enough number of people ask for the special crust that she was sure there was a fairly good market for gluten-free foods in Kittiport. The nit-picky part of her felt like she should have done more market research before ordering a whole new set of menus, but even if the new addition was a complete disappointment, the amount of money the store would be out would be negligible.

The sale of their very first gluten-free pizza brought a smile to all of their faces. Sometimes Ellie felt like it could be hard to innovate with a pizzeria, but if this new, healthier crust option ended up being a success, then there was no telling what they would be able to try in the future. She had the beginnings of an idea for a low-carb bacon crust, but she needed to do more research before she began playing around with it.

"Hey, Ms. P, your phone is ringing," Rose said, poking her head out from the kitchen as Ellie and Clara celebrated yet another successful sale of their new menu option.

"Shoot, I forgot to put it on vibrate," Ellie said. "Thanks for letting me know, Rose."

Just the other day she had reprimanded Jacob for leaving the volume turned up on his cell phone, so she was glad that he wasn't here to see this. Feeling a bit embarrassed, she hurried into the back and managed to catch the call before it went to voicemail. The caller ID told her it was her best friend, Shannon Ward.

"Hey, can I call you back in a few minutes? I'm just about to leave the pizzeria and I want to leave instructions with Clara and Rose before I go," she said, tucking the phone between her ear and her shoulder as she reached for the second to last slice of the pizza they had made for lunch.

"Ellie, you need to come over right now. Russell's been shot!"

Ellie's blood turned to ice. She put the pizza slice down, then sat numbly in the chair.

"Is he okay?" she asked, realizing how stupid she sounded as she said it. Of course he wasn't okay; he had been shot.

"He's in the hospital. James got the call because he's his brother, and he called me while he was on his way to go see Russell. All I know is that he's in surgery."

"What should I do?" Ellie bit her lip. She and Russell had been dating for only a few months, but she cared about him deeply. He was a good man, and a good sheriff. If something happened to him, it would affect not just her and his family, but the entire town.

"Can you come over and wait for news with me?" Shannon sniffed. She must have been crying. "It'll be better to wait together."

"Of course," Ellie said. "I'm on my way right now."

Shannon and James lived in a nice house in town. Ellie went over a couple of times a month for dinner, or just to see her friend. Never had the drive seemed to take so long as it did that day. Every other vehicle on the road seemed to be moving at a crawling pace. She tried to keep an eye on the speedometer—the last thing she wanted was to get into an accident and possibly hurt someone else—but it was hard to force herself to go slowly when all she wanted was to reach her friend and find out if Russell was going to be all right.

When she finally pulled into her friend's driveway, she saw Shannon standing in the doorway, waiting for her. She wasn't wearing a coat, but didn't seem aware of the cold. Ellie shut off the car and hurried up the steps.

"No news," Shannon said before she could ask. "Come on in."

The two women waited together at the kitchen table with untouched cups of tea until Shannon's cell phone finally rang. Ellie watched as her friend answered, and crossed her fingers under the table.

"Okay. Okay, that's good. Yeah, she's here. I'll tell her."

Ellie bit her lip impatiently as she waited for the other woman to hang up. It didn't sound like bad news. For the first time since hearing about the injury, she wondered how it had happened. When she first got the call, she had been too concerned about Russell to think of anything else, but now that it sounded like he was out of danger, a million scenarios seemed to play through her head at once.

"He's fine," Shannon said as she put down the phone. "He got shot in the leg. It hit bone, so he'll be out of commission for a few weeks and might have to deal with physical therapy to avoid having a limp, but James said the doctor expects a full recovery."

"Oh my goodness, that's great news," Ellie breathed. "I was expecting the worst."

"Me too," Shannon said. She shook her head, then grinned. "Well, now that we know our favorite sheriff is going to be okay, do you want to hit the store with me before we go and see him? James said he can have visitors after he wakes up from the anesthesia, so we have time to pick up a gift basket or something. Hospital stays are never fun."

"No, they aren't," Ellie agreed, thinking back to when she had suffered through a serious concussion in November. She had not enjoyed the hospital stay very much at all, and knew that Russell would go stir-crazy if he were kept there for long. With any luck, he would be out within a day or two to begin his road to recovery.

CHAPTER FIVE

"Give me about three hours," Ellie said. "I'll bring over pizza, some brownie bites, and two liters of whatever soda you want."

She hung up and shoved her phone into her pocket before glaring at the large box sitting in the snow outside of her car. The darned thing just didn't want to fit. She had to get to the pizzeria, make another batch of pizzas for donation, whip up something for herself and Russell, then actually drop off the donations and leave the community center in time to make it to Russell's by lunch. She didn't have time to wrestle with an uncooperative box.

"One more try," she sighed.

After finally managing to wedge it into the passenger seat, Ellie drove straight to the deli, keeping an anxious eye on the clock. She really should have given herself more time, but it would be doable if nothing else came up.

The weekly special at the pizzeria was a thin crust margherita pizza, with fresh herbs and thick slices of the best mozzarella cheese around. Ellie made up three of these to take with her to the community center, plus a few plain pepperoni pizzas, before turning her attention to the special dish she was planning on making for her and Russell's lunch—a bacon cheeseburger pizza.

She started with a Chicago-style deep dish crust. Instead of the normal red sauce, or even barbecue sauce, she slathered it with creamy cheddar cheese sauce. A generous layer of ground beef followed, to which she added finely chopped white onions and garlic, then a layer of the shredded smoked bacon cheddar cheese that she had discovered a few months back. It had quickly become a favorite topping at the pizzeria. Over this she sprinkled even more bacon in the form of finely chopped bits. She brushed the crust with butter and dusted it with garlic powder, then put the entire thing in the oven.

While it cooked, she cleaned up her workspace and replaced the dough that she had used up. She carried the pizzas for donation out to the car and made sure they were stable in the back seat before heading back inside to check out the bacon cheeseburger pizza. When she peered into the oven and saw the melted cheese lightly bubbling, she smiled. The delicious-looking, cheesy monstrosity was sure to cheer up the sheriff.

She hummed to herself as she drove over to the community center. She had been in a good mood ever since she and Shannon had visited Russell at the hospital earlier in the week. The relief of learning that he would be perfectly okay after spending some well-deserved time resting had been overwhelming. Her thankfulness seemed to leak over into the other parts of her life as well, making her upbeat even during the normally dreary tasks that she usually disliked, like doing the dishes.

Her humming stopped mid-note when she turned the corner onto the road that the community center was on and saw an ambulance and two police cars with flashing lights in the parking lot.

"What's going on?" Ellie asked as she approached a small group of people huddled on the sidewalk. She recognized Ronald, and a few of the other faces looked familiar but she couldn't place names to any of them. She had left her car running a few spots away, and as the cold air nipped at her face, she was already wishing that she was back inside.

"I don't know," one of the women said. "I just got here. The police asked me to wait, so here I am. They aren't letting anybody leave."

"I heard the janitor say that someone was hurt," someone else said.

"I don't see what could have happened," the first woman said. "Was it one of the workers, or someone coming here to collect donations?"

"No idea. I was hoping you would have an idea, Kristy. You're way more involved in this place than I am. Maybe Ronald knows something. Ronald?"

The second woman turned to look, but Ronald was gone. Surprised, Ellie looked around. She saw him marching towards one of the police officers. A moment later, he was talking and gesturing at the building. It almost looked like he was arguing, though she couldn't imagine what about. The officer took a step back and said something into his walkie-talkie. A moment later a second officer approached and guided the man away.

"What in the world was that about?"

"No idea. That Ronald is an odd one," Kristy said. "He hasn't said a word since I got here."

"I thought he seemed a bit off when I met him the other day," Ellie admitted.

"Oh, I remember why you look so familiar. You dropped off all of those pizzas, didn't you? I didn't get a chance to introduce myself before. I'm Tina."

"Ellie." They shook hands. "It's nice to meet you. Are you a volunteer, or do you work here? The woman who showed me around last time said that you were her roommate, but she didn't mention much more than that."

"Oh, you met Courtney. I work here. Courtney actually started volunteering here after I told her about this place. I know she's hoping to get a paid position sometime soon. Her heart's in the right place, but I think she's hoping for too much. We don't have a very high employee turnover."

The other woman, Kristy, snorted. "Yeah, unlike your roommate turnover."

"Kristy, I told you that Courtney and I are working things out. Lay off, all right?"

Ellie raised her palms. "I don't want to get involved in whatever this is. I just came to drop off some more donations. I'm going to go ask someone how long they think this will take—I may have to come back later."

She started towards a police officer—the same officer that Ronald had spoken to, in fact—but before she had gone more than a few steps, the doors to the community center opened. A man that she didn't recognize came out and stood on the top step. He raised a megaphone to his lips.

"All right, everybody come inside, please. No one leaves the premises until they have spoken to an officer."

"What happened?" someone shouted as they began milling towards the door.

"A woman has been found dead. Anyone who knew a Courtney Morgan, please come to the front of the line."

Beside Ellie, Kristy gasped and teetered. She reached out to support the woman. The look on her face was heartbreaking. With a pang, she remembered what Courtney had said during her last visit.

"The redhead in the corner is my best friend... Kristy."

CHAPTER SIX

E llie helped the grieving woman inside, then made a beeline for the one familiar face among the police.

"Bethany," she said. "What's going on? Who is that guy?"

"That's Detective Mendez," the female cop said. "He's interim sheriff while Sheriff Ward is on leave. It's bad luck that something like this happened now."

"What happened to the woman? I met her the other day. She seemed so nice."

"Sorry, Ellie, but I can't talk about it. If you get in line, I'll try to get you out of here as soon as possible. I know you're probably busy, but I've got to go by the book."

"I understand," Ellie assured her. As she walked away, she couldn't help but feel a bit disappointed that Bethany hadn't shared more with her. She had gotten used to special treatment from the police during her relationship with Russell, and she supposed that had spoiled her a bit. She would just have to wait to find out what had happened with everybody else.

The lines moved painfully slowly. A few minutes in, Ellie remembered that her car was still running and had to explain the situation to the officer at the door in order to go out and shut it off. When she came back in, she had to take up a position at the tail end of one of the lines. By the time she made it to the front, she was already late to go meet Russell.

The actual interview itself didn't take long. She gave her name and her reason for being there, and described her one and only meeting with the dead woman. She didn't know why the police were making it such a point to interview everybody—it seemed a bit extreme—but she went along with it and soon after was out of the building and free to go about her day.

"Hey, you."

She turned to see Ronald standing just outside the community center doors. He was standing with his hands in his pockets, hunched against the cold.

"Yes?" she said.

"You came with a donation, didn't you? We're moving the setup to the elementary school on Spruce Street. You can drop everything off there if you want."

"Thanks," she said. "I'll do that now."

The school was on the way to Russell's, thank goodness. She felt bad that the pizzas were lukewarm, at best, by the time that they got there, but at least they wouldn't be going to waste. She was still shocked by the news of Courtney's death, and kept trying to puzzle out what could have happened. The police must have a reason to suspect foul play, or else they wouldn't have held everyone for questioning. Ellie couldn't imagine who would want to kill such a nice woman, and in the middle of a food drive no less.

After dropping off the pizzas and the boxes of clothes, she made a beeline for Russell's house. She was sure he would want to hear about the murder scene at the community center firsthand, and with any luck he might be able to get some answers.

"I was beginning to worry about you," he said as he answered the door.

He was leaning on a crutch, following the doctor's orders not to put any weight on his injured leg. Ellie was still dumbfounded by how lucky he had been. He had been shot while pulling over a drunk driver in the middle of the night. The routine stop had descended into chaos when the driver of the vehicle opened fire on Russell before he even reached the car. According to the police report, five shots had been fired, but only one had hit the sheriff. Russell had called for backup, and he and his deputies had managed to get the

45

man subdued and handcuffed without anyone suffering other injuries.

She knew that he thought that he had been unlucky, but she believed quite the opposite. Any one of those other four shots could have hit him. Even the bullet that he took to the leg could have been fatal if it had been just a couple of inches to the side. It was terrifying to think how close he had come to dying.

"I got caught up in what happened at the community center," she explained. "Did you hear about that?"

He nodded, his brow creasing. "Liam told me as soon as they got the call. I should have guessed that's where you were."

"What happened?" she asked as she came inside. "All I know is that some poor woman was found dead."

"That's the gist of it," he said. "I haven't heard much in the way of updates, but from what I did hear, the janitor found her in the snow outside the rear entrance. Liam told me there was evidence of trauma, so the case is being treated as a homicide, at least until someone says differently."

"Why did they make everyone stay and get questioned by the police? They can't think we all had something to do with it."

"My guess is that my replacement—" Russell made a face, "is eager to prove himself. He's a younger guy, and I think he's hoping to run for sheriff a couple of towns over next year. If he solves this case quickly, it's going to look good for him. He probably didn't want to chance losing track of anyone who could potentially be a suspect. Once news about the death gets out, the person very well may try to flee. That's going to be a lot more difficult if the police already have their information."

"I'm sorry that you're stuck here while all of this is going on," Ellie said with a grimace. "I can't even imagine how frustrating that must be."

"One good leg ought to be enough to do police work," he grumbled. "But I suppose there are upsides, like hand-delivered pizza from the best place in town." He eyed the box with a grin.

"I'll have to heat it up first," she said apologetically. "It took me ages to get through the whole fiasco at the community center."

"I'll preheat the oven," he said. "I need to get used to using this darned thing, anyway." He waved the crutch around in annoyance. "I can't wait to testify against the guy who shot me. If he hadn't been so trigger happy, I'd be the one working this case right now. Mendez is a decent guy, but he doesn't know Kittiport like I do."

Ellie smiled fondly. Russell's deep affection for his town was endearing. She had the feeling that even though Mendez was the official lead on the case, Sheriff Ward just might do a bit of investigating on his own.

CHAPTER SEVEN

The news of the murder at the community center spread quickly through the town. Papa Pacelli's was a common place for teenagers to stop and eat after school, and Ellie overheard such a large variety of rumors about Courtney's death as she served tables that she had to wonder where the kids were coming up with this stuff. There were a few interesting theories in between the crazy ones, though. Personally, she was leaning towards believing the people who said the janitor had done it. After all, didn't murderers usually return to the scene of the crime?

By the time Friday rolled around, the rumor mill had calmed down slightly. Ellie, who heard most of her news from Russell—a far more reliable source than most people had—wasn't encouraged when the sheriff told her that no suspects had been named yet.

"Mendez has a couple of people on his list," he told her when she dropped off some Chinese takeout and a cup of his favorite coffee for him before work. "But they haven't found anything solid. The poor woman had massive internal bleeding. From the sound of it, the injury happened days before she passed."

"Why didn't she go to the hospital?" Ellie asked. "If someone attacked her, why wouldn't she say anything?"

"I don't know." He sounded frustrated. "Liam told me Mendez isn't even certain it's murder any more. She could have gotten injured accidentally somewhere. If she didn't realize the severity of what happened, or couldn't afford to go to the hospital, well…" He shook his head.

"In a way, that's even sadder," Ellie said. "If she knew that she was hurt, but couldn't find help… the poor woman. She seemed just fine when I saw her last week."

"She didn't mention anything about being in an accident?" he asked.

"Nope. She seemed happy. She introduced me to her friends and told me to find her if I ever wanted to volunteer there."

"Did she seem to have any issues with anyone at the community center? I'm not ready to take foul play out of the equation completely yet."

"From the little I saw, she seemed to get along with everybody."

They had already gone over all of this, but Ellie understood his urge to have every detail perfectly right. Every time they talked about

Courtney's death, she hoped that something would click, but it never did.

"I hate just sitting around and not being able to do anything," Russell grumped. "I'm never going to retire. I would go insane."

Ellie got to the pizzeria in time to help Clara and Iris with the lunch rush. Clara, who had previously met Courtney, seemed to have been especially affected by her death. It was hard to imagine that the two women were only a few years apart in age, but Courtney's life was already over. They both seemed so young to Ellie. No matter what had happened to the woman, her death was terribly sad.

"I'm going to take my break now. Can one of you cover?" Iris asked, snapping the pizzeria owner out of her thoughts. Ellie had been staring blankly at a pile of chopped onions for who knew how long. She could use a change of pace.

"I will," she said. "Clara, when you get a chance, can you get these onions in the fridge?"

She walked through the swinging door and into the dining area, wondering what had her so distracted today. It probably had to do with her conversation with Russell. When she had thought the woman's death was a homicide, it had been easier for her to process it. There was a clear right and wrong, and someone to blame. If the original theory of it being a homicide was wrong, that meant that Courtney had died because she hadn't been able to get the help that she needed. Considering that she had been volunteering for the food drive when she died, the thought was especially poignant.

When she heard the bell on the door, she looked up automatically to greet the new guest. She was surprised to see a familiar face. It took her a second to place the woman. When she realized who it was, she was even more surprised. Tina, Courtney's roommate, gave her a quick wave.

"Hi. Um, it's Ellie, isn't it?"

"You've got it. How can I help you?"

"Can I have a personal veggie pizza and a soda?"

"Of course. It will be about ten minutes. Feel free to grab your drink out of the fridge and wait in one of the booths."

Ellie kept her eye on the dark-haired woman. She was itching to go and talk to her, but wasn't sure how to go about it without upsetting her. *It must be so hard for her, losing her roommate like that*, she thought, *there must be reminders of Courtney all over their place.*

When Tina's pizza was done, Ellie carried it over and set it down on the table. Tina gave her a small smile of gratitude.

"Thanks."

"No problem," Ellie said. "And it's on the house. I know you were close to Courtney; it's the least I can do."

"Thank you," the woman said, this time with more feeling. Her lips began to tremble. "Sorry, I just wasn't expecting this. I've had so many people be upset with me ever since it happened. Half the town seems to think I killed her."

This was a new one to Ellie. "Don't take anything anybody says to heart. Once rumors get started they have a life of their own. Look, don't tell anybody I told you this, but I have it from a good source that the detective in charge isn't even sure her death was a murder anymore."

"Really? I didn't know that. I hope more people start to hear that. Things have gotten really bad. I can't even go to the community center anymore because people think I'm the one who did it."

"I had no idea," Ellie said. "I'm so sorry."

"Well, you can see why I'm tearing up." She gave a sad laugh. "It means a lot to have someone be nice to me for a change."

The dark-haired woman picked up the pizza and tucked her soda into her overlarge coat's pocket. She gave Ellie a tremulous smile as she left. Ellie beamed after her, but the expression faded quickly as the prickling of suspicion rose up in her. If enough people believed that Tina had killed Courtney to ban her from the community center, then they must have a reason. Was it possible that she had just given away a pizza to a murderer?

CHAPTER EIGHT

"Hey, crazy bird," Ellie said fondly to the big red macaw. The bird was on the back of the couch, and was sneaking ever closer to her, her eyes locked on the sandwich in Ellie's hands. Bunny was watching her just as hopefully from the floor.

It was a lazy Sunday morning, and so far, the three of them had spent it lying around in front of the fire, the bird and the dog content to doze while Ellie read. Nonna was in the kitchen, baking something yummy. Ellie had caught sight of chocolate chips and pecans when she stopped in to make her sandwich, and was hopeful that cookies were on the menu.

She had turned her encounter with Tina over and over in her mind, and winced mentally each time. Her biggest mistake had been telling the woman what Russell had told her—that Mendez wasn't certain Courtney's death was murder anymore. The sheriff had told her that in confidence, and she had been foolish to let it slip to someone who very well could be a suspect on the case.

Embarrassment had kept her from telling him of her slip-up so far, but she knew that she would have to be honest with him sooner or later.

Her phone buzzed. She picked it up to see a text message from Shannon. *Are you free? Meeting Karen for coffee in half an hour.*

Sure, she texted back. *I'll be there.*

That meant she was going to have to get dressed and make herself presentable for the day, but she had probably lazed around enough. It was nice to have the weekends off, but she always felt guilty on the days that she did absolutely nothing. Besides, she needed to talk about her concerns with someone other than Russell. He was a great guy, but saw the world in a very black and white way. Besides, Shannon worked for the local newspaper. If anyone would be up to date on the rumors surrounding Courtney's death, it would be her.

After letting her grandmother know that she was going to be in town for a while, Ellie tucked Marlowe back in her cage, tossed a treat for Bunny, and pulled on her winter gear. Her phone had buzzed loudly that morning with a warning about severe winter weather, but so far it was a clear, if frigid, day.

Kittiport was situated right on the coast of Maine. The town was cute and idyllic in the summer, with the fishing boats bobbing on sparkling waves and all the tiny little shops putting their best wares out for tourists. In winter, the town was just as beautiful, but in a different way. Snow sat heavily on well-insulated rooftops, and smoke rose from chimneys throughout the town. The forest of the large state park that encompassed a good portion of the land around town was made up mostly of white pines, and to Ellie it seemed like the town was surrounded by Christmas trees.

She enjoyed the view as she drove into town, glad for a sunny day even if the air was icy. The frequent thaws and re-freezings were beginning to wear on her. She was ready for winter to end, and spring to return. It was hard to imagine that in a few short months the snow would be gone for the year, and she wouldn't have to watch out for patches of dangerous black ice when she was driving to meet her friends.

After ordering a triple caramel latte, Ellie joined Karen at their regular table by the window. Shannon wasn't there yet; she had texted a few minutes ago to say she had been held up at work.

"Hi, Ellie," Karen said as the pizzeria owner joined her. "How is everything with you?"

Good," Ellie said. She sipped her coffee, then winced. Too hot. "Well, as good as can be expected. You've heard about the death at the community center?"

"I heard about it. Benton Harbor doesn't have much news of its own, so the paper prints stories from Kittiport a lot. Poor girl. It's sad that no one found her for so long. I heard her body was frozen by the time it was discovered."

"I met her just a few days before she died," Ellie said. "Russell said that according to the autopsy, she had probably been injured for a while before she succumbed to it. I can't stop thinking that she might have been suffering the entire time I was speaking to her. I keep wondering, why didn't she get some kind of help?"

At that moment, the door to the cafe opened and Shannon came in. She waved to let them know that she saw them, then walked over to the register to order her drink. When she approached the table, Ellie shifted her jacket off the chair to free up space.

"Sorry I'm late," her friend said. "One of the women I work with took a few days off because her friend died, and I've been scrambling trying to do both of our jobs. I don't blame her of course, but it's taxing."

"Wait, was her friend's name Courtney?" Ellie asked.

"Yeah," Shannon said. "The woman who died at the community center. Kristy—that's my coworker—was close to her."

Small world, Ellie thought. *Sometimes I forget how tiny this town is. When they say everybody knows everybody, they mean it.*

"We were just talking about that," Karen said. "No one seems to have any straight answers about what happened."

"The whole thing is such a mystery," Shannon said. "If someone attacked her, why didn't she report it? If she was in an accident, why didn't she go to the doctor? If that temporary sheriff, Detective Mendez, doesn't pin down a killer, we may never know."

"I did learn something else yesterday," Ellie said. "Courtney's roommate, Tina, came into the pizzeria. She told me that people seem to be blaming her for the murder. It's gotten to the point where she can't even go to the community center. My first impulse was to feel bad for her, but then I remembered something odd, an interaction between her and another woman, Kristy, who Courtney said was her best friend. Kristy seemed to think there had been some sort of disagreement between Courtney and her roommate. Do you think there might be something there?"

"Maybe," Shannon said. "If things were bad between them and they got into a fight, well, Tina might not even realize it if she hurt the other woman. It still raises the question of why Courtney wouldn't have gone to the doctor."

"Maybe there was someone she was protecting," Karen chimed in. "Did she have a boyfriend or husband?"

The two other women looked at each other and shrugged. There was too much that they didn't know. *I think it's high time I talk to Russell about what happened yesterday*, Ellie thought. *He probably knows why the rumors about Tina started, and he would definitely know if*

Courtney had a husband or boyfriend. She was sure the police had already investigated everyone close to the woman, but more minds working the case couldn't hurt.

CHAPTER NINE

Ellie returned home from her coffee date to find Nonna waiting in the kitchen with a plastic container full of cookies and her coat and shoes already on.

"What's going on?"

"I was hoping you could give me a ride to the community center, dear," the older woman said. "After everything that those wonderful people have suffered through, I thought it would be nice to do a little something special for them."

"The cookies? I'm sure they'll appreciate them." Ellie sighed. She hadn't planned on returning to the community center, at least not until after Courtney's unusual death had been solved. She had been face to face with a killer far too often for comfort. While she might enjoy speculating about the crime, she didn't want to get up close and personal if she could help it. She didn't see how she could say no to her nonna, though. "Let's bring another of those boxes of clothes from the basement while we're at it."

They arrived at the community center less than half an hour later. Bunny had come along for the ride, and was sitting happily in the back seat. Ellie was glad that she had thought to bring the little papillon. She hadn't gotten out of the house as much during the colder weather, and could probably use the change in scenery. As she parked, she noticed that it didn't look like it was as busy as it had been the first day that Ellie had stopped in. She wondered if that was because of the death, or because people had started to get back on their feet now that the electrical company had had a chance to repair the damage done to the power lines during the storm. She remembered the winter weather advisory that had popped up on her phone that morning. She would have to check the news later; hopefully they weren't in for another heavy snowfall.

"Nonna—wait—" Ellie hurried around to the passenger side of the car, where her grandmother was trying to pull herself up while holding both the container of cookies and her purse. "Let me get the cookies. And hold on to my arm. Everything that melted earlier this week refroze, and there are a lot of icy spots. You don't need to break anything else."

The two of them made their way carefully down the sidewalk and up the steps, with Bunny trotting at their feet. Nonna leaned heavily on Ellie as they traversed some of the worse patches, and the younger woman was reminded again of how old her strong-seeming grandmother really was. It scared her to think that the elderly woman would have attempted to make this journey on her own—and with her hands full, no less—if she hadn't stopped her. How could she stop her grandmother from constantly overestimating her physical abilities without insulting her?

It was a puzzle that she would have to solve another day. Right now, they had a batch of delicious home-baked cookies to drop off. Ellie pulled the door to the community center open and held it for her grandmother. The older woman walked inside ahead of her, and she followed closely behind.

"The donations go to a room down that hall," Ellie said.

"I know where I'm going," Nonna said, not unkindly. "Hand me the cookies. I want to bring them in myself. Arthur was dedicated to this place; I'm doing this for him."

Ellie handed over the plastic container and watched carefully to make sure her grandmother was steady. Thankfully, the slightly sloped hall had a railing, and the older woman was able to lean on this as she made her way towards the donation center.

The bulletin board caught Ellie's eye before she could follow. She glanced down at Bunny, who was sniffing around excitedly, as much as her leash would allow. It occurred to her that they probably didn't want dogs near the food donations. She had better check the pinned rules before going any further.

The rules said nothing one way or the other about dogs, so Ellie figured she and Bunny were probably safe. At worst, they would be asked to leave if it turned out dogs weren't allowed. She was about to turn and join her grandmother down the hall when a familiar name caught her eye. It was a handwritten ad for a new roommate, posted by someone named Tina Collins. She didn't know the last name of the woman who was Courtney's roommate, but she would have bet that it was the same Tina.

That was fast, she thought. *But I guess if she needs someone to cover the other half of the rent, it can't be helped.* Then she noticed the date on the paper. It was dated *before* Courtney's death.

Ellie frowned. She remembered Kristy's offhand remark about Tina's roommate turnover rate. It was obvious that there had been some sort of rift between the two roommates. She wondered if Courtney had been the one to decide to go, or if Tina had been kicking her out. Either way, it seemed like an important piece of information. She pulled out her cell phone and snapped a photo of the note, which she planned to send to Russell later. She knew that he was frustrated with his lack of involvement in this case; the note might at least give him something new to mull over.

CHAPTER TEN

When she reached the donation room at last, she found her grandmother deep in conversation with another elderly woman. She wasn't in a hurry, and she didn't want to interrupt, so she wandered over to the food table and snagged one of the cookies that Nonna had brought. Bunny seemed happy to be in a new place. She was on her best behavior, and seemed to understand that this wasn't the time or place for begging.

"If you were this good all the time, I would take you more places," she said to the dog. "Come to think of it, you've been much better behaved while we're out and about ever since you fell into the ocean last year. Did you learn your lesson when you almost drowned?"

The little dog wagged her tail, happy with the knowledge that her owner was speaking to her, even if she didn't understand what was being said. Ellie felt a rush of affection for the Papillon and bent down to stroke her back. She hoped the dog was happy, overall. Sometimes she felt like she was quite the boring owner. With the weather like it had been, they hadn't even managed to go on a daily walk lately.

"Cute dog. Is she friendly?"

Ellie looked up to see the redhead, Kristy, leaning against the food table. She looked tired. The last time Ellie had seen her had been on the day that Courtney's body was discovered. She remembered how shattered the woman had been when they had found out about her friend's death. She was glad to see that she was still getting out and interacting with people—it must be better than sitting cooped up at home.

"Yes, she is. You can pet her if you'd like. Her name is Bunny."

Kristy crouched down and held out her hand to the little dog, who sniffed it with a rapidly wagging tail. Ellie smiled as the other woman scratched the dog behind the ears. She was a firm believer in the healing power of pets. Animals seemed to have a way of making even the worst hurts better.

"Thanks. She's a cutie," the woman said, standing up. "I'm glad you stopped by again. We lost a lot of support after what happened to Courtney. It's not so bad now, since things are mostly back to normal, but we're going to need all the help we can get after this next storm blows through."

"I saw something about that this morning," Ellie said. "Is it supposed to be bad?"

Kristy nodded. "We're supposed to see high winds, freezing rain, and later on a couple of feet of snow. The whole shebang. Thankfully the weather looks clear for the foreseeable future afterward, but I'm sure there are going to be quite a few power outages before it's over. If the snow is bad enough, the grocery store might close, which means that anyone without a car is going to be stuck in Kittiport with no food. Even people who have a vehicle probably won't want to venture out until after the plows have come through. We're recommending to everyone that they stock up with at least three days of food and bottled water before the storm, and we're handing out free blankets to anyone that needs them."

"If the storm hits us that hard, I'll probably have to close the pizzeria," Ellie mused. "Thanks for the warning. I'll keep an eye on the weather channel."

"No problem. We just want people to be safe." The woman frowned slightly. Ellie guessed that she was thinking about her friend. She made a decision, based on what she would want if their positions were reversed. She would want to do anything in her power to find out what had happened to her friend, even if it was painful to think about.

"Kristy… I know this might sound like an odd question, but what do you know about the relationship between Tina and Courtney? I saw on the bulletin board that Tina had posted that she was looking for a new roommate, and the note is dated from before Courtney's passing."

"Tina… well, there is a lot of history there," Kristy said, her frown deepening. "It feels odd to talk about it, but I guess there's no point in keeping secrets for her anymore. After Courtney broke up with her last boyfriend, she didn't have anywhere to go. She stayed with me for a while, but I live in a tiny one-bedroom apartment with my fiancé, and there just wasn't enough room. She heard that Tina had a spare room and was looking for someone to share the rent with, and, well it seemed like a perfect match."

"It went sour?" Ellie guessed.

"It did. I don't want you to get the wrong idea about Courtney. She was an amazing person with the biggest heart of anyone. It's just that she was bad with money. Like, really bad. She started being late with her portion of the rent pretty much right away. She borrowed the cash from me a couple of times, but I have my own stuff I'm trying to work through and I just couldn't keep giving it to her. Eventually it got to the point where Tina had to put her foot down. She was going to let Courtney pay her only half of the money she owed, if she moved out by the end of the month, which would enable Tina to find another roommate sooner rather than later. I know

71

Courtney was looking for a better job, and was really hoping to get one here, but Tina just didn't think she would be able to find one in time."

"Wow," Ellie said. "I guess everybody has a lot going on beneath the surface. I would never have guessed any of that. Do you think the issues between the two of them might have escalated into a physical fight at some point?"

"I have no idea. Do you think that Tina could have had something to do with her death? I mean, I heard the rumors, but I think that Courtney would have told me if something violent had happened between them."

"That's what I'm trying to find out," Ellie said with a sigh.

Bunny started barking so suddenly that it made them both jump. She followed her dog's gaze to see Ronald approaching.

"Get the dog out," he said, sounding annoyed. "No pets in here. You have to leave her in the car."

"Come on, Ron, leave them be. The dog isn't hurting anybody. There's hardly anyone in here," Kristy said.

"The rules are the rules," he said. "Go on."

She apologized and tugged on the dog's leash. Bunny was still yipping, her tiny, fierce gaze fixated on Ronald. It took Ellie a second to pull her away. She caught her grandma's eye on her way out and nodded at the door. She would wait outside for the older woman to get done; she wasn't going to leave the poor dog alone in the car, not when it was so cold out. Besides, she didn't want to go back in and have to talk to Ronald again anyway. She understood that he was enforcing the rules, she just wished that he didn't have to be so rude about it.

CHAPTER ELEVEN

The promised storm failed to appear overnight. Ellie kept a close eye on the weather channel as she got ready for work that morning, but none of the weather reporters seemed to be able to agree on when exactly the northern coast of Maine was going to be hit. It looked like it would be safe to open the pizzeria as usual that morning. She could always decide to close early if it looked like things were beginning to get bad.

Mondays always meant a new pizza of the week. Considering her favorite chip dip, Ellie had designed an artichoke and garlic thin crust pizza with asiago and mozzarella cheese. She always enjoyed introducing a new type of pizza to the menu, but was especially in love with this recipe. It paired especially well with their gluten-free crust, and despite the looming threat of the storm, business was hopping.

Around three in the afternoon, the sky began to darken in a menacing fashion. Ellie had to double-check the clock; it was so dark that it appeared to be a few hours later outside than it really was.

"Jacob, I'm going to start telling people we aren't taking any more delivery orders. I don't want you to get stuck in the storm when it hits."

"All right, Ms. P. Do you think we're going to close early?"

"Let's see how things go. If we get freezing rain, we'll close up for sure."

A few minutes later, she got a text from Shannon asking if they were still open.

Yes. For now, she replied.

Can you put an order in for me? Deep dish supreme. I'll be there soon, Shannon sent back.

Will do.

Shannon showed up a few minutes before her pizza was ready. Papa Pacelli's was entirely empty by then, and just minutes ago, freezing rain had begun to fall, hard.

"This is terrible," Shannon said, shaking off her jacket as she came through the door. "Are you going to close early?"

"You're our last customer," Ellie said. "Everything I've been hearing tells me this storm is only going to get worse, and I want to be safely home before it does."

"Smart idea. Sorry if my order is holding you up."

"It's not a problem. We had one more, but they called to cancel. Did you get out of work early, too? You usually stay at the paper later."

"Oh, yeah, everyone got sent home. Half of the places in town are closed. You should have seen the line outside the grocery store, though. A lot of people are doing some serious last minute shopping."

"Wow. I'm glad—Hold on, sorry."

Ellie's phone was buzzing in her pocket. She pulled it out and saw Russell's number on the screen.

"I've got some interesting news," he said once they got their greetings out of the way. "I don't know much yet, but I thought I'd share with you since you've been just about as involved with this case as I have. Liam just called to tell me that Detective Mendez took Tina Collins into custody."

"Really? How did they link her to Courtney's death?"

"It's all thanks to that photo you sent me of her post on the bulletin board, looking for a new roommate. I passed it on to Detective Mendez, and he did some digging. It turns out that Tina's neighbors heard a lot of raised voices coming from her house in the days leading up to Courtney's death. One of them claims he heard Tina tell Courtney that she wished she would just disappear. A few days later, she was found dead. It's enough to raise eyebrows, at least. She'll be held for questioning, and the police will be searching her apartment for a possible murder weapon."

Ellie gave a low whistle. All of this because she had happened to glance at the bulletin board on her way into the community center. "Well, I'm glad to hear that the police have a suspect now. Thanks for letting me know."

"Thanks to that jerk who shot me, I now know what it feels like to be left out of the loop." He gave a dry chuckle. "It doesn't feel good at all. Hey, I hope you're closing early. I've got the news on, and it looks like Kittiport is going to be buried in a few hours."

"Yep, we're closing right now. Shannon's here picking up a pizza, and she's our last customer."

Her friend reached for the phone, and Ellie handed it over while she went into the kitchen to get Shannon's deep dish supreme boxed up and ready to go. When she came out, her friend handed the phone back.

"Sorry, I said goodbye and hung up without thinking. I don't know if he wanted to talk to you again."

"He'll call back if he has anything else to say," Ellie said. "Here's your pizza. Fresh out of the oven."

"Thanks." Shannon took the box. "I just checked with Russell and he said he's free. I was wondering if you wanted to have dinner with James and me tomorrow night, if the roads are safe. I'm guessing the whole town's going to have a snow day, so I thought it might be fun to use the extra time to do something fun while we're all off work."

"Sure. If the pizzeria's closed, my schedule is free," Ellie said. "I can pick up Russell, since he's not supposed to be driving. What time should we be there?"

"Six? If James and I don't have to go in to work, we can do it at any time, really."

"Six works for me. Should I bring anything?"

"If you could whip up something for dessert, that would be great."

"Something decadently sweet and loaded with calories. Got it. I'll do my best."

The next morning, Ellie woke up to find that the woods behind her grandmother's house had turned into a shimmering winter wonderland. The freezing rain had encased the branches in a thin coating of ice, and the snowfall that had followed later during the night had settled over everything like a fluffy white blanket. Every inch of the trees sparkled in the sunlight. It was gorgeous, though

Ellie knew that the frozen branches spelled disaster for the power lines.

Since the skies were clear, she guessed that the plows would have no trouble clearing the roads by that evening. Around noon, she decided it was time to tackle the task of figuring out what she was going to bring to dinner. Shannon had said dessert, but she hadn't specified what kind. Since she and Nonna were completely snowed in at the moment, she would have to get creative with the ingredients they had on hand.

"How about this?" Nonna asked, holding out a slightly stained recipe page. She had a huge binder full of recipes, from ancient-looking handwritten ones, to a mulberry pie recipe she had asked Ellie to print off for her last week. Ellie loved looking through the binder; she never knew what she would find.

"That looks amazing," she said. "Do we have all of the ingredients?"

"I think so. There's a stash of candy bars on the top shelf in the back. I'll get started on the crust if you want to do the filling."

The recipe for homemade chocolate chip pie was surprisingly simple. The graham cracker crust was ready in no time. Ellie finished melting down the marshmallows, then set the pot aside to cool while she whipped the cream and grated the candy bars. She folded all three ingredients together, then spread it over the pie crust.

Other than the whipped cream she would bring to put on top, that was it.

"That was easy," she said. "I hope it's good."

"I made it once a few years ago," her nonna said. "You won't be disappointed."

"Are you sure you don't want to come to dinner?" Ellie asked.

"No, no. I'm going to be much happier in front of the fire here. You know how early I go to bed. I would probably fall asleep at the table. You go and enjoy yourself, dear."

"Thanks, Nonna. I'll set a slice of pie aside for you."

CHAPTER TWELVE

"You look nice," Russell said as they pulled out of his driveway. "I'm sorry about this. I should be the one picking you up. I can hardly wait until I get the all-clear to drive again from the doctor. I'm itching to get behind the wheel."

"Do you know how much longer you have to wait before you can start doing all of the normal things again?" Ellie asked. "Kittiport needs its sheriff back."

"I should be able to stop using the crutch by Friday. It will feel wonderful to use my own two feet to get around again. I've been shot before, but it's never laid me up like this. It was just an unlucky shot."

Ellie grimaced and he chuckled.

"I know, I know, you think I'm lucky to be alive. But look at it this way—the guy was drunk, and it was dark out. He was shooting blindly. What are the chances that one of the bullets would hit my leg? Not very high."

"Either way, you have to admit it could have been worse."

Before the shooting, the danger that Russell put himself in every day hadn't felt quite real to Ellie. She knew he had devoted his life to catching the bad guys, but he had always seemed somehow invincible to her. Hearing the news about him getting shot had been a sharp reminder of reality for her. She knew that once he went back to work, she would be worrying about him constantly. It wasn't something she was looking forward to.

"I know." He fell silent for a moment, then changed the subject. "So, what's in the bag?"

"Dessert," Ellie said, smiling. "You'll have to wait and see to find out what it is."

"I'm okay with that sort of surprise," he said with a laugh. "I have to say, it feels weird to be completely off duty. I don't even know how long it's been since I wasn't on call. I'm not saying I *like* having Detective Mendez take over, but it is a good feeling to know I won't be called out in the middle of dinner."

"How is he doing on that case?" Ellie asked. "I haven't heard any news since your call yesterday. Did Tina end up confessing?"

"No, but she's still in custody," he told her. "They found some incriminating messages on her phone, but nothing strong enough to hold her for more than forty-eight hours. With any luck by this time tomorrow, Mendez will be able to press charges."

Ellie pulled into Shannon's driveway a few minutes later, feeling happier than she had in a long time. Everything seemed to be looking up. The police had a likely suspect in the murder case, Russell was doing better, and they had all just gotten through what looked to be the last big storm of the season unscathed. In a few weeks if they were lucky, it might start warming up for good. With the warmer weather came a whole new set of possibilities for the pizzeria, which she was excited to explore.

Inside, Ellie followed her friend into the kitchen while James and Russell caught up in the living room. Shannon's kitchen was modern and large, and Ellie was utterly in love with it. Her grandmother's kitchen was a good size as well, but it didn't have the smooth granite counter tops or the expansive island with a gas range that her friends did.

"Do you mind if I peek?" she asked, gesturing at the oven. "Whatever it is, it smells delicious."

"Go ahead. It will be done in a few minutes, anyway. I'm going to go get the wine from downstairs."

Ellie turned on the oven light and peered through the little window. Inside were bubbling stuffed pasta shells, topped with marinara. They looked delicious. Her stomach rumbled. This dinner was a phenomenal idea, and something they all needed.

It was beginning to get dark out by the time they were all seated around the table. There was more than enough food to go around, and Shannon urged them not to be shy about taking seconds. At first, they ate in silence, but once the sharp edge of their hunger had been dulled, the conversation began to pick up.

"How's the drive-through window working out for you?" James asked.

"It's wonderful. It really makes handling the pickups a lot smoother. Thank you so much for all of the work you did on it."

"I would have been happy to do the entire thing," he said.

"I'm glad she didn't take you up on your offer at first," Shannon said with a shudder. "It terrifies me to think what could have happened. The first person she hired got killed. It could so easily have been you."

"I don't like thinking about that either," Ellie said. "There have been too many close calls lately. Let's talk about something else. How has work been, Shannon? You stop in and visit me pretty often, but

I feel like I never get the chance to ask how things are going at the paper."

"Work is actually going pretty well," her friend said. "They have me doing a lot more now. I might be looking at a promotion soon, in fact."

"Really? You haven't mentioned that before," James said. "Congratulations. I hope you get it."

"It's nothing set in stone yet." Shannon frowned. "To be honest, I almost hope I don't get it. If the position opens up, it will be because the current employee is fired. She's been breaking company policy, but she has good reason."

"Is this Kristy you're talking about?" Ellie asked. "I remember you mentioned her the other day when we had coffee. I've spoken to her a few times. She seemed nice. What did she do to get in trouble?"

"Yeah, it's her," her friend said. "It's kind of a long story, but one of my bosses found out that Kristy has been skimming money from the newspaper. She's been there a long time, and the stealing only started about six months ago. If it was anyone else, she probably would have been fired on the spot, but my boss took her aside and talked to her to try to find out if something was going on. It turned out that her fiancé is an abusive jerk, and she's desperately trying to gather enough money to leave him. She got put on probation and was told to return the money. I know she was offered resources that could help her. She was given a second chance and a lot of understanding, but earlier today I heard that more money went missing. If it's her, I don't think she's getting a third chance."

"Wow," Ellie said. "I didn't know any of that.

Shannon nodded. "I feel bad for her, but I also don't think it's right for her to steal from the paper. We're like a family—granted, a pretty dysfunctional one—but it's not like she wouldn't have had help if she had asked for it."

Something occurred to Ellie. "Hey, when I spoke to Kristy last, she told me that Courtney stayed with her and her fiancé for a while. If the fiancé is abusive to Kristy, do you think it's possible he might have lashed out at Courtney, too?"

Russell frowned. "It's a possibility, but they would have had to have an altercation recently. She was injured a few days prior to passing, not weeks or months. I'll mention this to Mendez in the morning. It's possible that Tina didn't do it, of course, in which case they're going to be back at square one."

"Do you know if a guy named Ronald is on their list of possible suspects?" Ellie asked.

"The name sounds familiar," he said.

"He's one of a few paid employees that works at the community center," she said. "Skinny guy, balding. He was there the day that she was found, so I'm sure Detective Mendez took a statement from him."

"I really wish I was on this case," Russell said, shaking his head. "I don't know who you're talking about, but if you've got a reason to suspect him, I'll pass it on."

"I don't, really," Ellie admitted. "Other than the fact that he seems a little bit off, and Bunny doesn't like him. I know Courtney wanted to get hired there full-time, so maybe he felt threatened by her, like she was trying to take his job."

Shannon laughed. "I think you missed your calling, Ellie. You should have been a private investigator, not a pizza chef."

"Sorry," Ellie said, giving an embarrassed grin. "I can't help it. Who can turn down a good mystery?"

"I can," James said. "Right now, the only mystery I care about solving is what sort of dessert you brought."

"I'll go get it," Shannon volunteered. "You guys sit tight."

Ellie glanced over at Russell, who was tapping his fingers slowly on the table. She smiled when he met her gaze. She knew that he, like her, was still mulling over the mystery of Courtney's death. Maybe that was why she liked him so much; they were two of a kind.

CHAPTER THIRTEEN

The next day, even most of the rural roads had been cleared of snow and ice. That meant back to work for Ellie and everyone else in town. The city kept the sidewalks along Main Street clear, but they hadn't touched the parking lot behind the pizzeria. Ellie had hired a private company to come out and plow the lot in the mornings after they had received more than two inches of snow, but they didn't offer a salting service. As a result, the pizzeria's parking lot more closely resembled an ice rink.

After getting the restaurant ready to open, Ellie tackled the hard-packed, icy snow herself with a bag of salt. She was still salting the most traveled areas when Clara arrived, closely followed by Rose. She gave each of them a bright greeting on their way in. It was another sunshiny, beautiful day, and it had put her in a good mood.

When she got inside, she pulled off her coat and gloves and held her hands out to the warmth of the stove. The kitchen, which usually felt too hot once the ovens had heated up, now felt perfect.

"Man, it's good to be back in civilization," Rose said. She was sitting at the small table in the kitchen that they used for lunch breaks with her phone charging from the socket next to her.

"What do you mean?" Ellie asked, trying to remember if her employee had mentioned some sort of camping trip.

"We lost power during that storm two nights ago," the younger woman said. "A huge branch snapped off a tree under the weight of all of that ice and broke the power lines. The power company said it might be another couple of days before they get someone out to fix it. We've got a fireplace and stuff, so I'll be able to stay warm, but it still kind of sucks."

"A lot of people lost power again," Clara said. "I'm glad I didn't. I have a parrot, and he wouldn't be able to handle the cold."

Ellie felt a stab of guilt. She had enjoyed a delicious dinner in a warm home with her friends the night before, when there were dozens of people around town who didn't even have heat. She hadn't even thought of donating anything to the community center, even though there were still a few lonely blankets in the basement that they were never going to use and it would barely cost her anything to throw together some piping hot pizzas to donate to people who didn't have any way to heat up food on their own at the moment. She had liked the community center when she first discovered it, but had been eager to avoid it ever since Courtney's death. She realized that wasn't fair to the people who really needed the help. It looked like it was time for another delivery.

***

She arrived at the community center with a stack of pizza boxes a couple of hours later. The building was busier than ever. She realized a lot of people must be planning on spending the entire day here, and maybe even the night too. For people who had lost power and didn't have a fireplace or a generator, the low temperatures could be dangerous, or even deadly, especially for the young and the old. It made sense that families would want to spend the day somewhere with power, running water, food, and community.

Ellie walked down the hall to the room where all of the donations were brought. She looked around, but didn't see any familiar faces. A smiling older woman greeted her and thanked her for the pizzas.

"We'll just put them on the table right here," she said. "Is there anything else I can help you with?"

"Do you have a bathroom I could use really quickly?"

"Sure. Go out the door and turn right. The bathroom will be on your left, just past the kitchen. It's clearly labeled; you won't miss it."

Sure enough, Ellie had no trouble finding it. After attending to her needs, she paused to check her phone. She was hoping for an update from Russell about the case. Today was the day that they would have to either release Tina or charge her with something, and she felt anxious waiting for the verdict. Disappointingly, there was nothing from the sheriff. She reminded herself to be patient, and that even if something had been decided, he might not know about it yet.

She exited the bathroom and started back up the hallway, but paused after taking only a few steps. The sound of arguing had caught her attention. It was coming from the door marked *Kitchen.* She tried to convince herself it wasn't eavesdropping if they were talking loudly enough that she could hear them without even trying.

"We have gotten more complaints, Ronald." The voice was feminine and kind, but firm. Ellie thought it probably belonged to the older woman that she had just spoken to, but couldn't be sure. "I'm sorry to say, this is your last warning."

"Ms. Shippey, I need this job. And you need me. I know this place better than anyone."

"After multiple guests have come to me complaining about rudeness, I don't have much of a choice," the woman said. "I'm not trying to be mean. I've given you plenty of chances. Just think before you open your mouth, Ronald, please. The last thing we want is to drive people away."

"There isn't even anyone to take my place, now that Courtney is gone. I care about the community center as much as anyone. I've told you before, and I'll tell you again. I wasn't rude to those people.

It's not my fault if some people can't follow the rules, or can't read the signs."

"It's not your fault, no, but it's your *job* to correct them kindly. And please be more respectful when you speak of that poor woman. She was a wonderful soul, and I wished many times that I could have offered her the job that she wanted here."

"I knew it," Ronald said. He sounded hurt, more than angry. "You were planning on replacing me with her, weren't you?"

"We've gone over this, Ronald," the woman said. She sounded tired now, as if rehashing an old argument. "Yes, I was considering hiring Courtney when a spot opened up, but I wasn't looking to replace you specifically. Look, I'm sorry, but I have to be firm on this. Begin treating our guests with respect. This is your final warning."

Ellie jumped back and ducked into the bathroom seconds before the kitchen door opened. She leaned against the wall, going over what she had heard in her mind. Ronald had seemed fixated on Courtney taking his job. He was obviously very attached to working at the community center. If he really believed that the older woman, Ms. Shippey, was going to fire him in order to hire her, he might have taken extreme action. Was a job at the community center worth killing over? Ellie had a feeling that for Ronald, the answer just might be yes.

CHAPTER FOURTEEN

Ellie took out her phone and dialed Russell's number. She had a feeling that what she had overheard was too important to wait. Ronald seemed unstable, and if he thought that Ms. Shippey was going to fire him, then there was no telling what he might do.

The sheriff listened as she reiterated the conversation to him. She was a little bit embarrassed to admit that she had hung around outside the kitchen door to listen to the conversation, but her own pride was a small sacrifice to make if the information ended up saving somebody's life.

"I'll pass the information on," he said when she was done. "I just heard that Tina was released, so that means the killer is still out there. We can't be too careful. It seems that for a nice girl, Courtney had quite a few people who disliked her."

"The more I find out, the more shocked I am," Ellie said. "I guess most people probably have their fair share of secrets, though." She chewed on her lip, trying to think if there was anything else she wanted to say before she hung up. She was ready to get out of there and get back to the pizzeria, that was for sure.

"Oh," she said, suddenly remembering something from another of their conversations. "The other day, you said that Tina had incriminating messages on her phone. What were they about?"

He hesitated. "I suppose I'm not technically on the case, so I might as well tell you. They were messages between her and a friend. The friend asked how she was holding up, and she replied saying she was better than ever, and that she was relieved Courtney was gone. In the message, she said that she felt like a big weight had been taken off her chest, and that she was glad the house was her own again."

"It sounds like she's *glad* Courtney died," Ellie said, horrified. "She didn't seem happy when I saw her at the restaurant."

"She may have been faking her grief, if she was trying to get attention off her as the killer," Russell said. "Or, maybe she really does feel bad for Courtney and the messages were sent while she was under the influence of alcohol. Whatever the truth, it's out of my hands. I'll keep digging, but it's not your job and you should be careful."

With that, they hung up. Ellie knew that he was right. She had backed herself into a corner before, and didn't want to draw any attention to herself if she was right about the killer being someone from the community center.

She glanced at the clock on her phone. It was high time that she got back to the pizzeria. She slid the phone into her pocket, straightened up, and opened the bathroom door to find herself face to face with Ronald.

She let out a strangled yelp of surprise, then clapped her hand over her mouth. He took a step backward, and Ellie saw his arm tighten around the case of toilet paper he was holding.

"Sorry," she said. "You just surprised me, that's all."

He nodded curtly, then stepped aside so she could leave. She took a step forward, then flinched back as he closed in again.

"How long were you in here?" he asked.

"Why?" She hoped he wouldn't be able to tell that her voice was higher pitched than usual out of fear. "Is there a time limit on how long someone can use the bathroom?"

His eyes narrowed slightly. She saw them dart to the side, towards the kitchen door. To her horror, she felt a blush rise in her cheeks. His face flushed red.

"You were listening in, weren't you?"

"I didn't hear anything," she lied. "I don't know what you're talking about. Now, pardon me. I need to get back to work."

She tried to move forward again, but his thin body remained unmoving in the doorway. She fancied she could see the gears turning in his head.

"You're that lady with the dog, right?" he said. "You were one of the ones that complained to Ms. Shippey, weren't you?"

"I didn't complain to anyone," Ellie said honestly. "I left when you told me to, and this is the first time I've been back since. Now, will you please get out of my way?"

He gritted his teeth. What he said next came as a surprise. "I'm sorry for being short with you when you brought your dog in."

She blinked. "Oh. Well, thank you. Apology accepted."

"I know I'm not very good with people, but I love this job and I really need it. I know you heard my conversation with the owner. Just... don't say anything bad about me, okay?"

Ellie nodded. Ronald gave her a small smile. At that moment, someone called out his name.

"Ronald? What are you doing?"

She recognized Kristy's voice immediately. She heard the sound of footsteps coming down the hall towards them.

"There are a ton of people waiting for the game room to get set up. I thought you were going to organize that?"

Kristy reached the bathroom and looked surprised to see Ellie standing there. The pizzeria owner noticed that her eyes were red, as if she had been crying recently.

"I'm on my way," Ronald replied, back to his old, grumpy self. "I've got to drop off this toilet paper first. The janitor's late, and someone complained about empty toilet paper rolls in a couple of the stalls. Of course, it falls on *me* to take care of it."

"Well, sorry, I would have done it if someone had asked. You're the one that has the keys to the supply closet, though. Anyway, I just came down here to remind you about the game room. I need to get going, so I can't help."

"I'll walk out with you," Ellie said quickly, glad for an excuse to leave behind her strange encounter with Ronald. "I should be going too."

She bade the thin man a brusque goodbye, then started down the hall with Kristy. The other woman looked even more exhausted than before. Ellie didn't blame her. Her best friend was gone, she was suffering through an abusive relationship, and she had the threat of losing her job hanging over her head. The woman could probably use some kindness in her life.

"Hey, Kristy?" she said as they walked. "Do you want to get coffee with me?"

"Right now?"

"Sure, if you have time."

"Well…" the other woman hesitated for a moment. "Okay, I guess I do."

"Awesome." Ellie smiled at her. "My treat, as thanks for rescuing me from Ronald."

"Thank you." Kristy gave her a grateful smile. "Let me go grab my coat."

CHAPTER FIFTEEN

Ellie took Kristy to the same coffee shop that she went to with Shannon and Karen every week. She had been gone from the pizzeria for longer than she had intended, but she didn't regret making the offer. Kristy had been going through some truly horrible stuff lately, and though Ellie knew a cup of coffee wouldn't fix anything, she hoped that the act of kindness would remind the woman that she wasn't alone.

The table by the window that Ellie usually sat at was taken, so the two of them opted for a more private table near the back. Kristy was carrying a large tote, which she set down under the table before sitting.

"Are you going on a trip?" Ellie asked, indicating the bag with a nod of her head.

"Oh, no. I have my laptop in here, and I don't want to leave it in the car because of the cold."

"Ah, okay," Ellie said. She didn't really know what to say next. Her great idea had only extended to buying the woman coffee. She had no idea what they would find to talk about for the next who-knew-how-long.

"So, what was Randall bothering you about?" Kristy asked.

Ellie was glad for the conversation topic, and launched into the story enthusiastically.

"So, who's Ms. Shippey?" she asked when she was done. "I hate to admit it, but I don't have the slightest clue of how the community center is run."

"She owns the building. Her husband created some huge charity foundation before he passed away, and that's how she pays the employees and manages all of the activities we do there throughout the year," Kristy said. "She's nice. Probably a bit too nice, really. Randall's a weird guy. He got in trouble last year for kicking a kid out who was running in the halls. As in, he made the kid go outside and wouldn't let him back in. It wasn't some teenager or something like that, either, but a young kid that was there for our free daycare program. I'm surprised he didn't get fired right then."

"I'm surprised she kept him around after that," Ellie agreed. "I don't like the way he was talking about Courtney, either. It almost sounded like he was glad she's no longer with us because he thought she was trying to take his job."

"He did always act like he was in some sort of competition with Courtney. I think you're right; he felt threatened by her."

Ellie glanced around to make sure no one else was listening in before she spoke in a low voice. "You don't think he could have hurt her, do you?"

Kristy bit her lip. "It's a possibility," she said at last.

"The poor woman. I just feel so bad for her. The only reason I can think that she didn't go to the doctor, or report the crime if she got attacked was that she was protecting whoever did it."

She looked up to see tears sliding down Kristy's face. She kicked herself mentally. This wasn't the time or place to talk about Courtney's death. What had she been thinking? She had wanted to take Kristy out to cheer her up, not dredge up sad memories.

"I'm so sorry," she said, leaning forward to put a hand on the other woman's arm. As she did, her elbow knocked over the half-full cup of coffee. "Shoot. I'm going to go get napkins to clean this up."

She grabbed a wad of the cheap paper napkins that they had near the register and began wiping up the floor. The corner of Kristy's tote was touching the puddle of spilled coffee. Ellie reached out to move the bag aside, and was surprised when Kristy reached down and pulled it away first.

"I should be going," the other woman said quickly. She fumbled with the handle on the tote. Her hands were visibly shaking. Ellie couldn't believe how stupid she had been to bring up Courtney in the first place.

"I'm so sorry, Kristy. If you want to stay longer, I can buy another cup of coffee and we'll talk about something else."

"No, I really should get going. You're a nice person, Ellie. Thank you."

She stood up and began to walk away. Ellie saw the tote's shoulder loop catch on the corner of the table and opened her mouth to say something, but it was too late. Kristy felt the loop catch and gave the bag a firm tug to free it without looking back. The bag tore at the seam and the contents spilled out across the cafe's floor.

Ellie froze as a huge amount of cash fluttered to the ground around her. The entire cafe had gone silent. Kristy was staring down at her in mute terror.

"What —" Ellie began. She broke off mid-sentence as Kristy's fingers fumbled inside her jacket and a second later she pulled out a small revolver. Her hands were shaking too much for her to be able to aim it well, but the pizzeria owner didn't want to take her chances with even a randomly fired bullet.

"No one move." The words came out in a dry whisper. Kristy cleared her throat and tried again. This time her voice was louder and clear. "No one move."

"Kristy, what are you doing?" Ellie said. "Did you steal all of this money?"

"How do you know that?" the other woman asked, her eyes wide.

"A friend of mine works with you at the newspaper. She told me some of what's going on. This is all stolen, isn't it?"

"No," the other woman said defensively. "Not all of it. I saved up some. I had to hide it from Jayce. Cash was easiest."

"You need help, Kristy." Ellie was still kneeling on the floor, where just moments ago she had been cleaning up spilled coffee. She made to stand up, but stopped when Kristy centered the barrel of the gun on her.

"I don't need help," Kristy said. More tears were sliding down her face. "I don't need anyone. I just want to leave. Please, no one move. I don't want to hurt anyone else, but I will if I have to."

"Anyone else?" Ellie asked, worry clenching her stomach. "Did you already hurt someone, Kristy?"

The other woman's lips trembled. She closed her eyes. Ellie began to slowly push herself to her feet, but before she could make any progress, Kristy's eyes snapped open.

"Stay where you are," she said. "You've been nice to me and I don't want to shoot, but I will if I have to. I'm done being a doormat."

"Kristy—"

"Don't think I don't mean it," the other woman said. "I killed my best friend. Compared to that, this would be nothing."

Ellie was stunned into silence. Kristy was the one that had killed Courtney? Why? How? None of it made any sense to her.

"Empty out your purse and put the money in it. When you're done, hand it to me slowly, and stay on the floor. I'll leave, and none of you will ever see me again."

The contents of her purse clattered as she dumped it out on the floor. Her cell phone was so tantalizingly close, but she didn't dare make any moves towards it. Instead, she did as Kristy had requested; she began grabbing at the bills spread over the floor and shoving them into her bag. Out of the corner of her eye, she saw movement. One of the women sitting at one of the farthest tables had her phone out and was typing surreptitiously on the screen under the table. Ellie knew that she had to find a way to keep Kristy distracted.

"I understand about the money," she said softly. "You needed it to get away. And the gun—you needed it to protect yourself. But why would you hurt Courtney?"

"I didn't mean to," Kristy said in a tremulous voice. "I never knew how bad it was."

"What happened?" Ellie asked.

"She found out about the money. She didn't think I should be stealing. She wanted to go to Ms. Shippey for help. I told her if she did, then our friendship would be over. I was angry, and so was she. I got in my car and pulled away, but she stepped out in front of me. I tried to stop, but it was icy and I couldn't. I didn't even hit her that hard, but she ended up getting pinned between my car and another car. We both knew she was hurt. I was scared and I begged her not to tell anyone. She kept it to herself. The next day she seemed better, but the day after that she started getting sick, she said her stomach hurt... I asked her not to go to the doctor, for me, because I didn't want to get in trouble. We were at the community center when she started getting really bad cramps. She went outside for some fresh air. When she didn't come back, I thought she had gone to the doctor. I never thought—"

Kristy's voice broke as she began to sob. Hesitantly, Ellie stood up. The gun wasn't pointing at her any longer, in fact, the woman seemed to have forgotten all about it. She tensed for a moment when

FOUR CHEESE MURDER: BOOK SEVEN IN PAPA PACELLI'S PIZZERIA SERIES

Ellie touched her hand, but let the weapon slide from her grip without a fight.

"There, there," Ellie said feebly, patting her arm. Over the other woman's shoulder, she could see the flashing lights of the police cars through the window. Courtney's killer had been caught at last, but clearing up the mystery wasn't nearly as satisfying as she had thought it would be.

CHAPTER SIXTEEN

Ellie watched out the front window as Russell parked his truck behind her little green car. A smile grew on her lips as she saw him walk unaided across the driveway and up the path to the front stoop. He had a limp, but that would go away with time. She was glad to see him up and active again, and knew that he was happy to be back to his normal life as sheriff.

She opened the door before he could knock. Bunny let out a sharp yap and dashed over to dance eagerly around his feet. He bent down to pet her before straightening up to greet Ellie.

"You look nice," he said.

"It's a funeral, I'm not sure nice is the right compliment," she said. "Morose, maybe."

"Well, you look morose. In a nice way. Are you ready to go?"

"Yes, just let me say goodbye to Bunny and grab my purse. Do you know if we're still meeting Shannon and James first?"

"I believe so. I haven't heard anything to the contrary."

"Good," she said. "It will be nicer to go together. I still don't know if it's right for us to go. None of us knew Courtney that well."

"You should be there," Russell said firmly. "You're the one who found out who killed her. Her parents invited you specifically. Shannon has to be there to cover the story. And, well, I'm going because you asked me to."

"Thank you." She gave him a quick smile. "Let's get going, then. The last thing we want is to be late."

When the service ended, Ellie hung back near the grave while the rest of the gathering began to drift away. She felt an overwhelmingly deep sadness when she thought of the young woman and the life that she would never have. She didn't like it, but she felt sad for Kristy too. The other woman had made bad choices that had led to someone's death, and Ellie didn't doubt that she deserved whatever sentence the judge decided on, but try as she might, she couldn't forget the way the woman had just stood there and sobbed after confessing what she had done. She didn't want to feel pity for a killer, but it seemed unavoidable in this case.

"Do you need more time?" Russell asked from beside her. Ellie sighed, then shook her head. Standing there staring at a young woman's grave wouldn't achieve anything. It was time to go and give Courtney's family the privacy they probably wanted.

"Thanks for coming with me," she said to Russell as they walked back towards the car, where Shannon and James were waiting. "It means a lot."

"I'm glad you decided to go," he said. "I think it's better, in the long run. There are some cases that you just never forget. Getting this sort of closure doesn't fix everything, but it helps. Spending time with those close to you helps, too."

"I don't know how you do it," she said. "You've worked on so many murder cases. How do you still have any faith in humanity?"

To her surprise, Russell smiled. "That's easy. Because people like you exist, and people like Shannon and James. Good people. I'm not in this to catch the bad guy. I'm in it for them. To protect the good ones."

Ellie nodded. It was a fine line, but she thought it was an important one. It was the difference between living a life with love in your heart, and living a life guided by hate or vengeance. She had to remember to be that way herself more; to focus on the good things and the good people that she loved, because they were all that mattered in the end.

41411241R00066

Made in the USA
Middletown, DE
11 March 2017